Boobela
and Worm,
Ace
Detectives

Boobela and Worm, Ace Detectives

Joe Friedman

Illustrated by Sam Childs

Orion
Children's Books

First published in Great Britain in 2009
by Orion Children's Books
a division of the Orion Publishing Group Ltd
Orion House
5 Upper St Martin's Lane
London WC2H 9EA
An Hachette UK Company

1 3 5 7 9 8 6 4 2

Text copyright © Joe Friedman 2009
Illustrations copyright © Sam Childs 2009

A catalogue record for this book is available from
the British Library.

ISBN 978 1 84255 680 1

Printed in China

The Orion Publishing Group's policy is to use papers that are natural,
renewable and recyclable products made from wood grown in sustainable forests.
The logging and manufacturing processes are expected to conform to the
environmental regulations of the country of origin.

www.orionbooks.co.uk
www.boobela.com

Contents

Ace
Detectives

Boobela had taken a break from studying
to read a mystery story to Worm.

   She sighed as she closed the book.
It would be so much fun to be
a detective.

But detectives wore disguises . . .

and whatever disguise *she* wore
she'd look like what she was . . .
a girl who was a giant.

Worm saw Boobela's face fall.
"What's wrong?"

"I'm too big to be a detective,"
Boobela said, staring at the ground.

Worm looked at her with soft eyes.
It was hard for Boobela to forget that
she was different to other children.

He thought for a moment about what to say. Then he poked her hand with his head.

"Silly billy," he said. "You're not *too anything*. The reason you can't be a detective is that you still can't read maps."

"I can," said Boobela weakly.

"Never in a million years," asserted Worm.

Boobela raised her head. "I'm going to make you eat those words!"

Worm smiled to himself. "Won't. Can't."

Boobela rushed off to get the map of the city that her gran had sent. She was going to show Worm that she *could* map read. *And* be a detective.

Worm looked at the map. "First, let's go to the water tower." He showed her how to make sure the streets on her right and left were in their proper place. "Now you're on your own," he said, settling back into his travelling box.

Outside, Boobela turned right, walked three blocks, then turned left. She stopped to check the street signs, then headed right for another four blocks.

"The water tower should be right here," she said. She looked up from the map and there it was!

"Now to the Green River," Worm said.

"I should have bet you I'd win," said Boobela, feeling more confident. She made sure the water tower was in front of her on the map, and figured out the way.

This time, Boobela made a left turn when she should have made a right. Worm didn't say anything until Boobela realized her mistake.

"I've got it wrong," she said, dismayed.

"No problem," said Worm. "Just find where you are now, then figure out a new route."

Boobela checked the street signs, turned the map around, and traced a way to the river.

They set off again.

Suddenly, Boobela stopped. An image of Joey, whom she had met on the Belching Giant, had suddenly popped into her head. He was crying.

"Something strange just happened," she said. She explained to Worm how she'd thought of Joey.

"Maybe he needs our help," Worm suggested.

* * *

Joey answered the door. His face was streaked with tears, but he looked at Boobela and Worm with surprise.

"How did you know?"

"Know what?" Worm asked.

"Somebody's just stolen Geets!"

Boobela knew that Geets was Joey's black and white dog. "When did it happen?" she asked.

"When I was home for lunch today."

Boobela felt a chill. It seemed her special magic had led them to their first case!

"We'll find him," Worm said. "Show us where it happened."

Joey led them to a long, narrow garden which backed onto woods.

"That's where Geets was tied," said Joey, pointing to a large post.

Boobela walked over. Worm looked down from her shoulder. There wasn't much to see, just a thick post with half a dog lead tied to it.

"We have our first clue," Worm said. "The dognapper cut the lead. Why didn't he unhook it?"

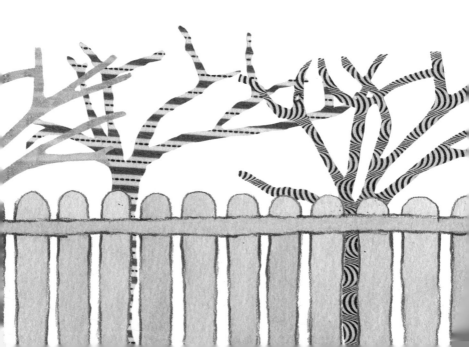

Boobela hadn't even noticed the lead was cut. She worried that Worm was going to be a better detective than her.

Taking out her new notebook she asked, "Did you notice anything suspicious?"

"Footprints? Anything left behind by the dognapper?" added Worm.

"No," said Joey sadly. "It's all my fault. I left him for fifteen minutes. I shouldn't have eaten so many biscuits for pudding."

"You didn't know there was a dog thief around!" protested Boobela. "Why don't you go inside while Worm and I start detecting?"

* * *

Worm sniffed the ground. "I smell leaf mould. But there are no trees here."

Boobela pointed to the woods at the back of the garden. She leaped over the fence and galloped around, trying to find clues.

"Slow down," laughed Worm.

Boobela realized a detective had to be slow and careful at times. She stopped running and started to inspect the ground little by little.

"*That's* more like it," said Worm.

Boobela bent down to pick up a thin strap of leather. The ground all around it had been trampled. This was a major clue!

"It's from a camera!" Boobela said, excitedly. "The dog thief must have taken pictures so that someone else could see what Geets looked like."

"That means there are least two dog thieves," Worm concluded.

"It also means the thief must have come here twice," Boobela added. "After he'd shown the photos to the second dognapper, he would have had to return to steal Geets."

Worm nodded. "Good thinking."

Boobela felt pleased. She wasn't as careful as Worm but she *did* have good ideas!

"Let's find out where he stood the second time," Worm added.

"There," said Worm, pointing his head. "*Stop!* You'll destroy the evidence. Put me down. And keep watch."

Boobela watched as Worm slowly crept over the ground, tasting the soil every few minutes.

Then she caught sight of a black bird sitting in a tree above them. The bird had its eye on Worm.

Boobela stood up. She knew this bird wanted Worm for dinner.

Before she could make a loud noise to scare it away, the bird dived. Towards Worm.

Boobela moved swiftly to
cover Worm with one hand and
shoo the bird away with the other.

"Caw, caw," screamed the bird.

"Whew!" said a shaken Worm.
"That was close. See this?"

Boobela leaned over. "It's a
footprint!"

"Yes!" said Worm. "And this?"

Boobela knelt down and picked up
some brown soil.

"I can taste rhododendrons in it. The same flowers that were at Scarlet Lake!"

"Barber Park!" Boobela and Worm said at exactly the same time.

* * *

"So," Boobela explained to Joey, "we know there are two people involved and one of them lives near the park."

"That's amazing," said Joey. "I had no idea you two were such ace detectives!"

"Actually, *I'm* the ace detective," said Boobela.

"Actually, *I'm* the ace detective," said Worm.

"I don't care which one of you is the detective, as long as you find Geets."

"We're off to the park," declared Worm.

* * *

Boobela ran all the way. She wanted to catch the dognappers and bring Geets home that night.

A tall woman with two dogs arrived at the park.

"Sorry to bother you," said Boobela. "We're doing a spot of detecting!"

The woman's dogs sniffed Boobela's feet. "What are you looking for?"

"Dognappers," said Worm.

The woman turned pale. "More than ten dogs have disappeared in the last month! I've lost two, which is why Barney and Lily are on leads. Everyone is using leads around here now."

"That must be why the thieves have gone elsewhere!" exclaimed Boobela.

After the woman hurried off, Boobela asked, "Why would anyone need so many dogs?"

Worm shook his head. "It's not for anything good. How can we find the dognapper?"

Boobela remembered seeing a picture of a man who was dowsing with a map.

"Maybe I could map dowse …"

"Great idea," enthused Worm.

They decided to lay the map on the bench and have Worm crawl from street to street. Boobela would check each street in turn.

"Long Avenue?" Worm read.

The rods swung wide. No!

"Philips Lane?" No!

"Barber Crescent?" The rods crossed.

"That's it!" exclaimed Boobela.

By the time they got to the crescent it was dark. So no one saw Boobela stopping in front of each house. The rods didn't say "yes" until almost the last one: number forty-eight.

"I want to catch him now! Let's ring the doorbell."

Worm shook his head. "We'll come back tomorrow morning. Maybe he'll lead us to his partner."

Boobela thought for a moment. "We'll have to get here early," she said. "And I'll have to be in disguise."

The next morning, Boobela got up while
it was still dark so she had time to find
the right clothes. Worm helped.

Boobela dressed
as a clown . . .

a balloon seller . . .

. . . and a princess.
"No, no, no," said
Worm. "We may be
following him all
day. You've got to
be invisible, or
at least as
invisible
as a
giant can be."
Finally, they agreed.
Boobela would dress as a postman.

"I look boring!" Boobela protested.

"That's the idea," said Worm.

They watched number forty-eight
all morning before a short, thin man
emerged.

His left hand was bandaged and he
was carrying a big canvas bag in his right
hand. They heard a muffled bark from
inside it.

"He's got a dog already," exclaimed Worm. "Maybe it's Geets."

"Look," Boobela whispered urgently. "His hand! That's why he cut Geets's lead – he *couldn't* unhook it!"

The man hurried down the street. Boobela followed, but not too close. As they arrived at the main road, they saw the man get on a bus. It pulled away from the kerb.

"We'll lose him!" Worm shouted.

"Not if I can help it!" said Boobela.

She crossed the street and ran, just managing to keep up with the bus. After twenty minutes, she was sweating and exhausted.

"I don't think I can go much further," she gasped.

"He's standing up," Worm encouraged. "Maybe he'll get off at the next stop."

He did. Boobela ducked behind a
delivery truck. When she looked up, she
couldn't see him anywhere. In a panic,
she rushed to the corner. There he was!
Going through a red front door.

Worm said, "I think we should get
all the other people who have had dogs
stolen."

"And surround the house?"

"Yes, with the police," said Worm.

Boobela had been tired, but now that she knew she was about to solve her first case she had bags of energy. "I'll do it!" she exclaimed.

*　*　*

Boobela returned an hour later with Joey, two policemen, and a group of dog owners from Barber Park. One of the policemen led the dog owners to the back of the house.

Boobela, Joey and the other officer rang the bell. Someone peeked from behind a window.

A moment later, there was uproar in the garden. The thieves had tried to escape!

The officer at the front said, "Let's kick in the door!"

Boobela and the policeman *kicked* at the door. It *smashed* to pieces!

"I've always wanted to do that!" exclaimed Boobela.

The noise triggered off dogs' barking . . .

. . . which led them to the basement, where they found twelve dogs in cages.

"Geets!" cried Joey.

"Sadie and Beano!" shouted the woman from the park.

There was a chaos of excited dogs, jumping on happy owners.

The two dognappers were put in handcuffs and led off by the police for questioning.

"Quiet!" shouted Joey, holding Geets in his arms. A hush fell. Geets licked Joey's face. "Which one of you is the detective?"

Boobela and Worm looked at one another. Then they smiled. "Both of us," they said together.

Joey continued, "Let's give a big clap to Boobela and Worm, ace detectives."

The dog owners cheered and the dogs barked. The noise was deafening. Boobela and Worm were *very* proud. It was fun solving mysteries!

The
Challenge

Worm tunnelled towards Hannah's compost heap. He had decided it was time to tell Hannah the truth. The truth about his family.

Halfway there, he remembered it was Sunday. Hannah would be having lunch with her family. He'd have to tell her, and the other Longworms, at the same time.

At the compost heap, he asked the first worms he met where he could find Hannah's family.

Dad pointed. "Over there. They had a lovely rotten mango saved up for Sunday dinner."

Worm thanked him and crawled further. Hannah saw Worm first.

"Worm!" she exclaimed. "How nice to see you!" Then she saw the serious expression on his face. "Is something wrong?"

By now, everyone in Hannah's family had stopped eating. They were all staring at Worm: her father, mother, sisters and brothers.

Worm thought it would be best
to introduce himself. "Hi, I'm Vivian."

"Vivian's a nice name," said
Hannah's mum, who seemed warm
and friendly. Hannah's dad, on the
other hand, looked very fierce.

Hannah introduced her parents and brothers and sisters, but Worm was too nervous to catch their names. He knew he'd better speak quickly. Otherwise he might lose his nerve.

"Hannah . . ." he began.

Hannah's mum gave her dad a meaningful look.

Worm's words tumbled out of his mouth. "I didn't tell you the truth when I first met you. The thing is, I liked you so much I didn't want you to hate me because I'm a Smartworm and I thought if you got to know me you might like me and then being a Smartworm wouldn't matter so much!"

Hannah saw her mum and dad looking at each other – and her big brother getting very angry. She knew she had to act quickly.

"I knew you were a Smartworm," she said, to Worm's complete surprise. "Most of the worms in your heap are. The idea that all Smartworms and Longworms hate each other is ancient history."

She turned to her mum and dad. "I know you two are far too clever to care about stupid things like that!"

Hannah's father had been ready to tell Worm to go away and never come back. Clever Hannah had put him off! For the moment.

Hannah's mum joined in. "I think you're a very brave and honest worm to come and tell us all this. A lot of worms would have been scared to do that."

Worm smiled weakly. He could see Hannah's mother was on his side. The truth was that he *had* been scared. But he'd done it anyway.

It wasn't over yet. Hannah's father hadn't spoken and her brother looked very upset.

"I can see you're brave," her father began. "But I've never had much time for Smartworms."

Hannah interrupted. "Please, Daddy," she pleaded. "Give Vivian a chance."

Worm could see her dad was torn. He wanted to say more but he didn't want to upset his daughter.

"I'll let it go for today," he said.

Worm then looked to Hannah's brother. He'd disappeared . . .

Worm stayed to get to know Hannah's family better. He talked about his favourite race, the One-Metre Tunnel, with her dad. They discussed tactics and the prizes they'd won. But all the while Worm wondered where Hannah's angry brother had gone.

"It's time for me to leave," he said.

Hannah accompanied him to the bottom of the compost heap.

"I'm very proud of you," said Hannah.

"I just wanted things to be straight between us," said Worm. Then he blushed. Why did he do that?

"Now they are."

"I hope everything is all right with your family," said Worm.

"I think you've won over my dad," she replied.

"And your brother?"

"It's only when he gangs up with my cousins you need to worry. They bring out the worst in him." This thought worried Hannah. "I'll check where he went."

She gave Worm a peck on the cheek and disappeared into the heap.

Worm tunnelled home. As he got near, he relaxed.

It was then he ran into them. A gang of worms. Hannah's brother was amongst them. The others must be her cousins. They looked very tough.

"We don't like Smartworms," said Hannah's biggest cousin. "And we *especially* don't like Smartworms who try to be friends with Longworms."

"The Broozer is right," agreed Hannah's brother. "We're going to teach you a lesson."

Worm made himself look big and got into his fighting pose. Worm had been taught by one of his uncles how to head box, but even *he* said worms weren't made for fighting. They were too soft. He knew he didn't have a chance against a whole gang. He had to think quickly.

"Who is your Challenger?" he asked.

"Challenger? What do you mean?" asked the Broozer.

"I thought," said Worm, "that you were all Longworms and proud of it!"

"We are," said Hannah's brother, feeling uncertain.

"Then," said Worm, "you must accept a Challenge from a Smartworm."

One of Hannah's brainy cousins explained.

"We'll choose the strongest and smartest of us. Our Challenger gets to ask the Smartworm a riddle. If he answers it, the Smartworm names a test of strength."

"That sounds complicated," said the Broozer. "Why don't we just beat him up?"

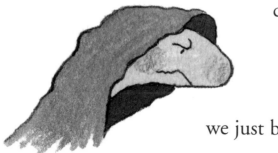

The brainy cousin spoke again. "Because if we refuse a Challenge, our families will be ashamed."

He looked at everyone. "You know our dads like to do everything by the rules."

They nodded, and huddled to pick their champion.

Worm felt pleased. He had a good chance against any other worm, one on one.

Eventually the gang chose the Broozer.

"You go first," said Worm. "You have to give me your hardest riddle."

The Broozer thought. And thought. And thought. Then he smiled. "I've got one you'll never get," he said. "What do you call it when worms take over the world?"

Worm didn't know this one. But he couldn't say that because he'd lose and he'd never see  Hannah again. So he concentrated. His brow creased with effort.

"Give up?"

Worm shook his head. He focused even harder. Then he laughed.

"I know," he said. "When worms take over the world you call it Global Worming!"

The Broozer's face fell. "That's right!"

"Now it's my turn," said Worm. "I choose Neck Wrestling."

Broozer's gang smiled. They were sure Worm didn't have a chance.

Worm planted his body firmly into the ground. His Challenger laughed. "Afraid I'm going to push you around?"

"Of course," said Worm. "You're very big and strong." He wanted the Broozer to be overconfident.

"Too right," said the Broozer. "Too strong for you."

The two worms locked necks.

"One . . . two . . . three. Start," said Hannah's brother.

Immediately, the Broozer tried to push Worm down. But Worm had guessed this would happen and was prepared. He braced himself, gave way a little, then resisted.

The Broozer said, "I almost got you!"

He pushed Worm one way, then another. He was *very* strong.

Worm wouldn't be able to last much longer. What could he do? Then he had an idea.

"Neck Wrestling is all in the mind!" he said confidently. "I always know what you're going to do next."

Worm thought his confidence would confuse the Broozer, and that he'd try to figure out what he meant. He waited until he felt the pressure against his neck get weaker.

Yes! This was his chance. He anchored the bottom half of his body in the ground and pushed with all his might. The Broozer was off balance and distracted. Worm pushed him all the way down.

"I won," he shouted.

"That's unfair," protested the Broozer. "I was thinking."

"Ah," laughed Worm. "In Neck Wrestling you have to think and push at the same time."

"You won fair and square," said Hannah's brother. "Congratulations."

And he shook Worm's tail.

At this moment, Hannah, her other brothers and several cousins arrived at the compost heap.

"You're in real trouble," said Hannah to her brother. Then she looked at her cousins. "That's not very fair: five against one!"

Hannah's brother hung his head. "That isn't the worst of it. Vivian challenged us and won."

Hannah looked at Worm with new respect. She gave him a kiss.

Then she nipped her brother's cheek.

"Ouch," he said.

"Get used to it," said Hannah. "You're going to be getting a lot more of that. From me and from Mum once I tell her what you did."

"And Dad will be angry I lost," said Hannah's brother, seeing a bleak future.

"Be gentle with him," said Worm. "He's done me a favour."

Hannah's brother looked at Worm with surprise. "No Longworm will ever bother me again."

Hannah chuckled. "It's true! And all their friends will give them a hard time when they realize they've lost a Challenge!"

Worm felt a bit sorry for them. But he guessed it would teach them a lesson. He had a very sore neck. But the look Hannah had given him more than made up for it!

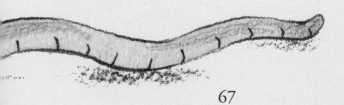

A Letter from Mum and Dad

Boobela saw the postman across the street. She felt she just couldn't wait any longer. She ran.

Is this what you're looking for?

Dear, dear, Boobela,

It seems like ages since we've seen you. We wonder if you've grown. I hope not! We've been here with our medicine man for more than a month already. We're still learning a lot but can see that we will need to move on soon. Just a couple more stops before we can come home. We'll make them as fast as we can!

The sight of her mother's handwriting made Boobela feel warm inside.

Boobela wondered how long a couple of more stops would take.

We've asked your Uncle Neill if he could come and visit for a while.

Uncle Neill is coming!

Is he nice?

He's ... like a whirlwind!

Boobela showed the pictures to the postman.

He'll come next month, so we've asked Gran if she could visit. You should see your dad now. He has a beard like Santa Claus (but fortunately, it's not white). I of course look exactly the same. (Just kidding...)
xxxooo
Mum and Dad

She's quite a character.

Boobela just wished her mum was with her. She nodded, unable to speak. Worm noticed.

We'd better let you get on.

Boobela walked home, carrying her precious letter.

The Family
in the Swamp

Boobela didn't mind mess, but she hated mud. She also hated rotting plants and flying insects. So the Smelly Swamp was the last place in the world she wanted to be. Especially on a day when all her friends at the Balloon Club were going on a lovely trip to a castle.

But Gran had asked her to find a plant she needed to cure Granpa and this plant could only be found in the Smelly Swamp . . .

Boobela put on her wellies and
looked up at the sun. She sighed.

"Goodbye," she said, dramatically.
"I may not be seeing you for a while."

She stepped
into the swamp.
At first she
couldn't see a
thing. Then her
eyes got used to the dim
light. She could see muck, fallen trees
and leaves drifting on the dark water.

When she tried to walk, the sludge
almost sucked off her wellies.

"At least it smells lovely," Worm said.

Boobela rolled her eyes. The mud
and rotting plants smelled like a
vegetable pizza that had turned green
and mouldy . . . disgusting.

Boobela squelched through the mud. Insects flew around her, biting every bit of flesh they could find. Soon, she was covered with oozing, squidgy brown mud.

Still worse, she hadn't seen any sign of
the plant Gran needed. And she had
to find it quickly.

"What's that?" Worm asked.

Boobela stopped and listened.
It sounded like . . . singing.

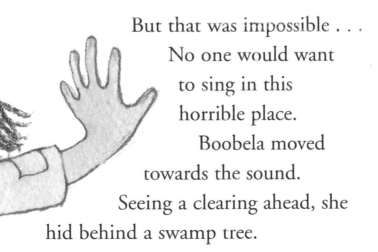

But that was impossible . . .
No one would want
to sing in this
horrible place.

Boobela moved
towards the sound.

Seeing a clearing ahead, she
hid behind a swamp tree.

Two muddy boys were dancing and singing. A woman was playing a flute cut from a plant, and a man kept time with a drum made from a large gourd.

Boobela stepped from behind the tree. The boys noticed her first. The youngest hid behind his mother's legs. She stopped playing.

"Hi," said Boobela, raising her hand in peace. "I'm Boobela and this is my friend Worm." Worm waved his head.

The man looked at Boobela warily. "We don't get many visitors here."

Boobela giggled. "I can understand that. It's a bit out of the way."

A dark look passed over the man's face. Boobela realized he hadn't been joking.

"I'm looking for some plants for my Gran," she added quickly.

"Why does she want plants?" the older boy asked.

"She's a healer. I'm learning to be one too."

"I'm afraid we can't help you," said the man. He waved Boobela away.

"Wait, Charles," said the woman. "She's just a child. The boys would love to play with someone new."

Charles whispered, "She's a giant! What if my brother has sent her to harm us?"

Boobela's sensitive ears picked up what the man said. And what the woman replied:

"She's a child with a worm as a friend. Worms are good creatures."

After a pause, Charles spoke. "My wife Helen sees only good in people. I hope she is right about you. You can stay with us until you find your plants."

Boobela said seriously, "We won't be any trouble."

Charles replied, "That's good. We've seen enough trouble."

Boobela was full of questions. Why was this family living in the swamp? What had happened between Charles and his brother? Why was Charles scared she would harm him? But she said nothing and simply bowed. Somehow it seemed the right thing to do.

Charles bowed back and smiled.
At this, the two boys came running up
to Boobela.

"How did you get to be so big?" asked one.

"I want a
worm friend,"
demanded the other.

Boobela bent down and gathered the
boys in her arms. "First things first.
What are your names?"

"I'm Curtis," said the smaller boy.
"And this wart is my brother Felix."

Curtis dodged away from Felix's attempt to kick him. Then he stuck out his tongue.

"What plant are you looking for?" asked Felix.

Boobela repeated Gran's description.

"Easy peasy!" exclaimed Curtis. "I call it Felix's Smelly Armpit! I know where to find some."

Curtis led Boobela and Felix into the swamp. Boobela couldn't get over the number of insects. Then she realized they weren't bothering the boys.

"Why aren't you being eaten alive?" she asked.

Felix took something out of his pocket. Boobela saw that it was made up of yellow flowers that had been crushed together.

"Rub this on your face," said Felix.

Boobela did. Immediately, the flying insects stopped bothering her.

"That's amazing."

"We tried about five hundred plants before we found this one," Felix told her. "Before that, the insects drove us crazy too!" They came to a patch of furry, weedy-looking things.

They were as tall as Curtis. Of course, Boobela was twice their size.

"This doesn't look like the one Gran wanted," Boobela said.

"It's not," said Curtis. "I'm hungry." He pulled a big red root out of the ground. Felix produced a pocket knife and cut the skin from the root. He handed it to Boobela.

"Have a taste. We call it swamp radish."

It looked a bit lumpy but now that she thought of it, Boobela *was* hungry. She took a small bite. It was good! "Yum," she said. She ate the rest. The children started to peel and eat the radishes.

After a few minutes, Worm shouted, "What about me? I need some dry soil."

"And what about Gran's plant?" Boobela said. "I need to find it quickly."

"Hold your horses," said Curtis. He turned to Worm. "Your food is just ten minutes walk away. And Felix's Smelly Armpit is—" Curtis dodged away from Felix "—another half an hour."

The boys led them to a small patch of dry soil. Felix picked some up and put it on Worm's box.

"Try this!" he said.

Worm did. "It tastes rotten . . . very nice!"

Felix put a handful of soil in his pocket. "For later," he promised.

Boobela was worried there wouldn't be enough time to find the plant for Granpa and get it to Gran.

"We need to hurry," she said.

The sucking mud and fallen trees made their progress slow. At last, Curtis pointed at a stand of plants. Boobela recognized them from her Gran's description. She picked a large handful.

Felix looked up at the sky. "It'll be dark in an hour."

Boobela was dismayed. "It's too late to get the plants to Gran!"

"We'll go first thing in the morning," Worm said swiftly. "I'm sure that will be all right."

"I hope so." Boobela turned to the boys. "We'll have to spend the night."

"Yippee!" Curtis did a little dance. "A sleepover!"

On the way back, Felix and Curtis grabbed some plants for dinner. Their mum cooked them in a stew. To Boobela's surprise, it was delicious.

There wasn't much to do after dark so it was straight to bed. Curtis wanted Boobela to tell him a story. Boobela remembered how her parents told her about their travels and adventures.

Boobela began: "Once upon a time there was a very lonely and sad girl who was a giant." Then she told Curtis and Felix how she met Worm. By the end, the boys were smiling sleepily.

Boobela lay down and pulled a blanket over herself and Worm. Charles came over. "Helen was right about you. I'm sorry I was suspicious."

Boobcla wanted a bedtime story too. "Why are you living here?"

Charles thought for a moment. "I was once a very rich prince. My father was the lord of the manor and my brother and I worked on his farm. We lived in a house as big as a castle."

"I thought we were all happy. But my brother wanted the castle and farm all to himself. He stole my father's crown and told him that I had done it. Soldiers were sent to capture me. I was warned just in time and we fled to the Smelly Swamp. We've lived here ever since."

Boobela thought for a moment. "I'm going to find your father and tell him he was wrong about you!"

Charles looked at her gravely, then laughed. "You *are* a brave girl. But I think coming to the Smelly Swamp was the best thing that ever happened to me. I spend all my time with the people I love, instead of working on the farm."

It was good that Charles was happy in the swamp. But Boobela was still determined to help him as she drifted off to sleep.

* * *

The following morning everyone woke as soon as it was light. Boobela hurried to get ready so she could bring the potion plants to her Gran.

Suddenly, she stopped. "I just remembered one of my dreams. I was flying over a huge field. It had wheat and some beautiful black and white cattle. I could see a large house in the distance. It had a flag with a dragon and a shield on it." She looked at Charles. "In the dream, I knew it was yours!

"I flew through a window into a huge room. There, on a beautiful red cushion, was a gold crown with rubies on all the pointy bits. A man with a grey beard was sitting next to it."

Boobela suddenly became aware that everyone was staring at her. Charles had turned pale.

After a long silence, Charles spoke. "How did you know about the cattle and the flag with the dragon and shield?"

Boobela was stunned. She said . . .

"Do you mean there really are cows and a flag like that?"

Helen nodded.

Boobela felt a bit scared. "When I went to sleep, I wanted to help. I guess I found a way to do it in a dream!"

Charles turned to the boys. "My father has found his crown. So he must know I didn't steal it. It's time for us to go home."

They cheered and had a big hug. Fortunately, the boys didn't want to kiss Worm. They're more sensible than girls, he thought.

Boobela said goodbye and charged off to her balloon.

When Boobela got home, there was a beautiful white horse standing in the road. A soldier dressed in a blue uniform waited for her at the door.

"You must be Boobela. I was told you were tall for your age." He handed Boobela an envelope.

Inside was a child's picture of a beautiful castle and a note from Curtis.

We are home now thanks to you.
You must come and visit us.

There was also a longer note, written in very formal handwriting.

Your dream was true. My father found his crown in my brother's room. He welcomed me home with open arms. My father and I have forgiven my brother and we are all living together again.

I enjoy having clean clothes more than I thought, but I will not forget the lessons I learned in the swamp.

If you ever need any help, you can call on me.

Your friend, Charles

"Please tell Charles that I got the plants to my Gran in time and that I'm glad everything worked out for the best. And let Curtis know I'll come and visit soon."

She and Worm watched as the messenger galloped off on his horse.

"Who would have guessed a trip to the Smelly Swamp would end like this?" she asked.

They opened the front door, glad to be home.

The
Inspection

Boobela had come to the harbour early. The ship carrying Gran and Granpa was due this morning. Boobela liked watching boats. Especially the ones from faraway places.

These were places with hairy spiders as big as Lassie and snakes that were big enough to swallow an ordinary person (but not her, of course!).

Worm wasn't so keen on harbours. He hated water and the thought of choosing to ride in a flimsy wooden shell didn't make any sense to him.

Boobela spotted a small sail coming into the bay from the north.

"There they are," she shouted.

"How do you know?" said Worm, who couldn't see anything more than a tiny bit of white.

Boobela tapped her nose with her finger. "Magic," she said.

Worm frowned. Boobela talked about her special powers all the time now. "You're becoming a magic bore."

"You're just jealous," replied Boobela.

Worm rolled his eyes. Well, he'd tried. He was sure Gran would put a stop to this. She didn't go on about *her* special magic all the time.

Gran and Granpa sat down in the rickshaw Boobela had borrowed. She lifted their suitcase and put it in the back.

"My special magic told me which ship you were on," Boobela said proudly.

Worm looked at Gran to see what she thought of this. She pursed her lips. Boobela didn't notice because she was inspecting Granpa. She could see he was feeling a lot better.

"You look great," she said, pleased. "Those plants I brought from the Smelly Swamp must have done the trick!"

"Not at all. It's all down to that wonderful porch you built for me," he said, laughing.

"Are you sure it's nothing to do with Gran's potions?" she teased.

"Potions, shmotions," replied Granpa. "I think she just gives me those foul-tasting things because I forgot her birthday last year."

"Keep laughing, Ben," said Gran.
"As soon as we get home, I have a list of
chores an arm long for you to do."

"I'm looking forward to it," Granpa
replied and he gave Gran a kiss.

Worm looked away. He hated
kissing. Most of the time, anyway.

Boobela pulled the rickshaw through
the streets. She took Gran and Granpa
past the new football stadium, the
outdoor cinema and the market.
Everyone looked at them, of course.

Rickshaws were rare and ones pulled
by a giant even rarer. But Boobela now
knew people didn't mean any harm.
Gran smiled.

When they got home Boobela helped Gran and Granpa get settled in their room. Then they all ate the lunch she'd prepared the night before: a homemade leek and potato soup, a vegetable lasagne and carrots and broccoli on the side.

After lunch, Gran said, "That was wonderful! Do you eat like this all the time?"

"Not *all* the time," replied Boobela carefully.

"We do eat lots of fruit and vegetables," Worm continued. "It's so we can keep the compost heap filled."

"Ah, the famous compost heap," said Granpa, who had heard the story of Boobela and Worm's bet. "Let's see it."

Boobela gave Gran and Granpa a tour of the garden. She pointed out how there were no sweet wrappers or weeds – "Worm is very fussy about these things" – and they noticed how well-kept the lawn was.

"I lie on it a lot, thinking," Boobela explained.

But Boobela's pride and joy was at the back. She had planted her own herb garden.

"Oh my!" Gran exclaimed, when she saw the flowers and herbs. "It's beautiful. You've got everything you need to make potions here!"

Boobela beamed. She and Gran chattered on about plants.

Granpa was more interested in the compost heap. He opened it up, pulled up his sleeve and then stuck his arm deep inside.

"Not too wet, not too dry. It's lovely and warm and full of worms," he said. "I couldn't do better, and I've been making compost heaps for ages!"

Back in the house, Gran checked out Boobela's bedroom and kitchen cupboards, and then they all sat in the living room and had a cup of tea.

"You have kept the place really well," Gran said to Boobela. She looked at Worm. "Since she met you, she's been much tidier."

"It was a bit messy . . ." admitted Worm.

"Let's see where you are with your reading," Gran said.

Boobela brought out all the books she was reading and showed Gran how far she'd got with them. Gran took notes.

"I feel like you're doing an inspection," commented Boobela.

"Sort of," acknowledged Gran. "Your mum and dad asked me to come down and see how you were."

"But I told them I'm fine," Boobela protested.

"Yes," said Gran, "but some children might say that so they didn't worry their parents."

Worm defended his friend. "Boobela wouldn't lie."

"She's doing amazingly well," agreed Gran. "It's unusual for a ten year-old to be so responsible!"

Boobela felt annoyed that her parents hadn't believed her.

"I think you deserve a reward for being so good," said Granpa. "And I deserve a treat for getting better. What can we do to have fun?"

Boobela thought for a moment.

"I know just the thing!" she enthused. "Fabulous Fun Amusement Park."

Fabulous Fun had dozens of roller coasters and other rides. Boobela had been dying to go there for years. Her parents were not big fans of thrill rides.

Then she thought how ill Granpa had been . . .

"They have some very scary rides. Are you sure you'll be all right?"

"Ask my doctor," said Granpa.

Gran twinkled. "He'll need a treat before he tackles that list of chores . . ."

"Wait a second," said Worm. "I can't go on a roller coaster. I don't have any bones!"

Gran laughed. "I do have bones but being thrown from side to side doesn't appeal to me either. You and I can watch Ben and Boobela make themselves sick!"

* * *

Boobela could hardly contain her excitement as she parked the rickshaw. The park looked amazing. "I want to go on that one first," she burbled. "No, *that* one!"

Then Boobela had a very depressing thought. "What if I'm too big?"

Granpa stuck out his jaw. "Nothing's going to stop me or my granddaughter from having a great time today," he said.

Granpa charged up to the gate and demanded to speak to the manager.

"This is Boobela," he said. "She wants to ride your biggest roller coasters."

The manager looked up at Boobela. "Well," he said, scratching his chin. "She'll have to duck a few times . . . but I don't see why she shouldn't."

Granpa smiled and shook the manager's hand.

Boobela jumped up and down. "Let's start with the biggest," she said.

Granpa shook his head. "If we work our way up, the last rides will be the best!"

Boobela thought that made good sense. They held hands as they ran to the first roller coaster.

Even though this roller coaster wasn't the tallest or fastest, Boobela and Granpa laughed like drains when they were turned upside down. They went on it three times in a row.

The first time Boobela almost hit her forehead on a beam when the roller coaster doubled back on itself.

The second time she remembered at the last second that the beam was coming, and the third time she ducked in plenty of time.

They examined all the roller coasters carefully before choosing again.

It was very tall, but only half the size of the one next to it. The carriage took for ever to climb to the first drop.

Then it seemed to stop at the top. Boobela and Granpa looked at each other and held on tight.

* * *

Granpa wanted to ride again but Boobela wanted to go on the tallest roller coaster.

"We can do that one twice!" she urged.

When they got to the top of the first hill, Boobela looked down. Even though she was twice the size of everyone else on the roller coaster, she felt very small. The roller coaster started to plunge.

She and Granpa screamed all the way to the end of the ride. Then they ran to the back of the queue to go on again.

After this, they went on a pirate ship that swung from side to side, higher and higher, until they thought they were going to fall out.

Over dinner, Boobela told Gran about how her special magic had shown her that Tom was in trouble and also what ship she and Granpa were on.

"I'm becoming a special magic genius," she said.

Gran said gently, "We want you to be full of magic, not full of yourself."

Boobela felt punctured. She looked down at the ground. Worm had been trying to tell her this for ages but she'd been too much of a know-it-all to listen. "I was just so pleased to be good at something," she said.

"And so you should be," said Gran. "I'm grateful every day that I've been blessed with the power to help people."

Boobela saw that it was better to be grateful than to have a big head. But she still couldn't look at Worm.

"It's something we all go through," said Gran. "When we first discover we can do something we think *we're* wonderful. But when we're older and wiser, we think we're lucky, which is even better."

Boobela looked up. "I'm lucky to have such a great Gran and Granpa," she said.

"And we're lucky to have such a brilliant granddaughter," replied Gran.

"Who wants to go on The Freefall?" asked Granpa.

"Me!" yelled Boobela. And the two of them ran off like little kids.

They got into the Freefall cage. Boobela's head almost touched the roof.

"You'll have to try to stay in your seat," Granpa said. "Otherwise you'll get a sore noggin."

Boobela nodded. The cage started to rise slowly.

Worm shuddered. "Better them than me." Then he smiled at Gran. "You're a good teacher, you know."

"It takes one to know one," smiled Gran.